This

The Waldo

Hon

Ben Douglass

FIRST EDITION
Mercury Flats Publishing
Portland, Oregon USA

Mercury Flats Publishing is a Portland, Oregon based sole proprietor business (DBA #1056590-98) that manages the intellectual properties of Ronald Dwayne Douglass, also known as Benjamin Douglass, Ben Douglass and Dizzy Douglass.

ISBN – 13: 978-1537082707
ISBN – 10: 1537082701

Front cover photo credit: Lucerne Valley Market, Lucerne Valley, California, taken by author September 2015.

Printed in the United States of America

DEDICATION

James Steven Shubin
1954 – 2002
Vacaville, California

A brilliant pianist and composer; a compassionate and
loving human being who died so very young and never
got that second chance at life. I was lucky to have been
his friend before he got really sick, and will always
cherish the time we did spend together and all the
wonderful memories.

Prologue:
A Desert Canticle

"It may never have occurred to you, but in my observations of this subject, I came to learn that nearly every great civilization evolved from a desert area. Our sciences, mathematics, astronomy and chemistry, had their beginnings in a desert land. Our alphabet and even the major religions of the West were born in desert regions. So, there must be something about desert life that is conducive to cerebral activity, a stimulant to thinking on the part of man. Maybe it is the broad horizons, the silent solitude of big, open spaces, the enormous starry night sky that stimulates expansive thinking or creates big ideas. The great Pythagoras (6th century B.C.) said, 'Go to the Desert, or it will come to you.' What he meant was, that if you don't get out to the desert periodically, to get yourself re-oriented, your mind will become like a barren desert."

Mojave Desert Ramblings
Sewell "Pop" Lofinck
1966

"The Mojave Desert is a land of weird and wonderful sights. Gangly plants that salute as you walk by. Sleepy, slow moving tortoises. Black cinder cones against gleaming white lakebeds. Wavering mirages on the horizon. Rivers that never enter the sea. An extreme land of snow, cold, wind, heat, salt, sand, of colors, forms, and distances that defy anything comforting or familiar. A land where you can stand at 282 feet below sea level and face a mountain screaming two miles straight up in front of your eyes, where you can be cotton-mouthed from the heat in the daytime, and longing for a warm down sleeping bag at night. A land of endless, open space. A land where some people come for no reason other than to be alone."

Mojave Desert: American Deserts Handbook
Rose Houk
2001

"The desert, any desert, is indeed the valley of the shadow of death."

Slouching Towards Bethlehem
Joan Didion
1965

"In the desert, there is all – and yet nothing….God is there, and man is not."

Passion in the Desert
Honore de Balzac
1896

"Men and women who are at her mercy find it hard to see in Nature and her works any symbols but those of brute power at the best and, at the worst, of an obscure and mindless malice. The desert's emptiness and the desert's silence reveal what we may call their spiritual meaning only to those who enjoy some measure of physiological security."

Tomorrow and Tomorrow and Tomorrow
Aldous Huxley
1956

"The desert says nothing. Completely passive, acted upon but never acting, the desert lies there like the bare skeleton of Being, spare, sparse, austere, utterly worthless, inviting not love but contemplation. There is something about the desert that the human sensibility cannot assimilate. I am convinced now that the desert has no heart, that it presents a riddle which has no answer, and that the riddle itself is an illusion created by some limitation or exaggeration of the displaced human consciousness."

Desert Solitaire
Edward Abbey
1968

"To those who do listen, the desert speaks of things with an emphasis quite different from that of the shore, the mountains, the valleys or the plains. Whereas they invite action and suggest limitless opportunity, exhaustless resources, the implications and the mood of the desert are something different. For one thing the desert is conservative, not radical. It is more likely to provoke awe than to invite conquest. In intimate details, as when its floor is covered after a spring rain with the delicate little ephemeral plants, it is pretty. But such embodiments of prettiness seem to be only tolerated with affectionate contempt by the region as a whole. As a whole the desert is, in the original sense of the word, awful."

The Voice of the Desert
Joseph Wood Krutch
1954

"The weird solitude, the great silence, the grim desolation, are the very things with which every desert wanderer eventually falls in love. You think that very strange perhaps? Well, the beauty of the ugly was sometime a paradox, but to-day people admit its truth; and the grandeur of the desolate is just as paradoxical, yet the desert gives it proof."

The Desert
John C. Van Dyke
1901

"As interesting and provocative as the cultural geography might be, the desert may serve better as the backdrop for the problematic relationship between man and the environment. The human struggle, the successes and failures, the use and abuse, both noble and foolish, are readily apparent in the desert. Symbols and relationships seem to arise that stand for the human condition itself. It is a simple, if almost incomprehensible, equation: The world is as terrible as it is beautiful, but when you look more closely, it is as beautiful as it is terrible."

Desert Cantos
Richard Misrach
1987

"The geographical, geological, and other natural history features of our desert domains are so varied and with them are bound up so many entrancing problems that twenty years of intimate acquaintance and wide travel over the arid Southwest have not desiccated my ardor for continued study and wide wandering nor lessened my eagerness to lead others to the heart of my kingdom of joy."

The California Deserts
Edmond C. Jaeger
1933

The month was July; the year was 1992

The United States officially recognizes three new republics after Yugoslavia breaks up; George H.W. Bush and Boris Yeltsin proclaim a formal end to the Cold War; former Panamanian leader, Manuel Noriega, is sentenced to 40-years in a U.S. prison on drug charges; four Los Angeles police officers are acquitted for the beating of Rodney King, which causes a week of violent rioting; the U.S. Supreme Court reaffirms the right to abortion; Caspar Weinberger is indicted in the Iran-Contra affair; unemployment is at 7.5 percent; album of the year is 'Unforgettable' by Natalie Cole with Nat King Cole; best academy award picture is 'Silence of the Lambs'; a 7.4 earthquake hits the area, the sharpest in 40-years, surrounding high-desert communities hit by dozens of aftershocks; temperatures soar, smashing a decades old record.

1

The desert can be a mysterious place as well as an unforgiving place; it can be a place that changes and evolves with a sudden rush of wind, a flash flood or a spectacular display of light. It can be a place of great suffering that cannot be avoided. The desert can also be a place of breathtaking beauty that seems to emerge out of nothing. Whatever the desert is or becomes we can choose how to cope with it, find meaning in it, and move forward with a renewed purpose. So it is with the Mojave Desert in California; in a small corner of Western San Bernardino county, located at the heart of state route 247, in a tiny, dusty town called Lucerne Valley.

The gentle breeze blowing from the east was hot, the kind of hot that causes your lips to crack without some form of protection. The air was so oppressive that most living things stayed where they were, unless it was absolutely essential to move. The only movement was human litter nudged slowly by the breeze. It was already late evening and the temperature hovered around 96 degrees with 100 percent humidity. There would be little sleep tonight without a working A/C.

Ruby May Broyles sat in her shiny, state-of-art, silver SUV, in the parking lot of the motel, with windows up, A/C on high, while sipping a grapefruit soda pop and pulling heavy drags off a cigarillo. The engine was running and sad country music blared from the CD player. Ruby looked briefly in the rear-view mirror and saw someone she barely recognized.

A pasty white face without make-up, framed by long, dull red hair with prominent streaks of gray, stared back at her. The once bright and rich brown eyes had lost their lustrous glow. The vacant stare made her feel uneasy and she quickly averted her gaze to the motel building. Her attention slowly moved over to the ragged neon sign at the office that flickered on and off.

This place in the middle of nowhere was called the Roach Motel & Café. As she stared at the sign she gave out a short loud laugh and shook her head. She remembered the day she arrived at this godforsaken outpost nearly one year ago. She remembered it like it was yesterday. She had asked the owner that first night why he named his motel the Roach?

The owner's incredulous response to her question was: 'Why shouldn't a man put his name on his business? It's a matter of pride.' Obviously the man had no sense of marketing, let alone aesthetics. And when she checked in that first night she had asked: 'Is there a better room available?' The owner simply chuckled and said: 'This ain't the Waldorf Astoria, honey! This is as good as it gets.'

Tonight was a similar evening like that first day she arrived last summer – hot and oppressive. Ruby originally left Denver, Colorado and was on her way to nowhere in particular, but seriously thinking of driving into the lower Baja Peninsula. The thought of living in a foreign country and not speaking the language however, dissuaded her of that idea quickly after much thought from reading travel brochures.

Renting a room at the Roach was a needed refuge far away from all her troubles. She had parked her SUV in the parking lot with the intention of never driving it again on the open road. Three times weekly like clockwork, she would sit in it, run the engine for forty-five minutes, listen to music, think about her life and get away from the heat. She often thought about the Roach as a last refuge of scoundrels. And she was not much different from all the other losers staying there – in fact, she fit in almost too well. The thought made her shudder.

Ruby's monthly room and board took $1200 of her $2000 monthly social security check, with the rest left over for soda pop, smokes, personal essentials, and clothes. The motel owner was kind enough to cash and manage her check for her. It's not that he looked upon her as special but he did this for other long-term residents as well. He seemed to be a father figure to most of the people that stayed there. As he told Ruby once: 'I collect people that no one else wants.' And by the looks of the current residents that statement was emphatically true.

The people at the Roach did not live. They just survived and passed the time of day, every day in a grinding monotony, waiting for something to happen, anything to happen. In the end not much happened, just another boring day and night in the desert. In fact, the last big exciting event for the motel and town was the arrival of the mysterious well-dressed lady from Denver. Ruby was the talk of the town for many months.

Nights like this forced her to think of her former life packed with family, friends, the theater, charity events, concerts, and dinners at Denver's nicest and priciest restaurants. She had married into one of the city's well-known pioneer families, and benefited greatly from all the social and political connections that came with such status.

For twenty-three years she had been the Chief Financial Officer of North American Trucking with an annual salary and benefit package of $800,000. She moved in powerful circles; wining and dining with state senators, judges and millionaires. She was so entrenched in the political life of the city and state, friends and colleagues started suggesting she run for political office – a few powerful and well-placed friends said she had more than a good chance to be Denver's next mayor, if she wanted it.

Her drinking finally destroyed all that. After her third DUII in seven years, and causing life threatening injuries to a pedestrian – who happened to be the daughter of the state's Supreme Court Justice – she spent three-year's in a minimum-security facility. She lost her job and her driving privileges were revoked for life. Her financial loss was devastating. She lost her 401K, investment portfolio, and other bank accounts, to pay off high-priced lawyers, court fees, and a huge victim's compensation package. The young woman she hit ended up a paraplegic.

To make matters even worse, her husband served her with divorce papers on the day she was released from jail. Her wealthy and well-connected friends turned away from her as if she had never existed. For two-year's while on supervised parole she studiously met all the requirements the state put upon her, including residential and outpatient treatment. Like others in deep denial about her drinking, she figured out ways to drink without being caught and played the system rather masterfully.

The last of her money was finally drying up and she couldn't bare it any longer living in Denver. She was finally free to go where she pleased. She went to the auto storage facility where her SUV was kept and well cared for. She paid her bill and realized she only had $2500 in cash, left over from her original legal settlement, for traveling money. Thank God she had the foresight to start drawing her social security early. She hopped in her car and drove out of the Denver city limits, never looking back or saying goodbye to anybody. At sixty-five this was her retirement, her golden years. 'Golden years my ass,' she said loudly.

For the first two months on arriving at the motel she spent a considerable amount of time nursing a bottle of Chivas Regal in her room. When she got tired of drinking alone, she would hang out at the Y saloon a few blocks down the road. The Y was a sports bar with two jumbo TV screens which was a favorite of truckers, bikers and locals. Ruby became an iconic figure at the Y in a short time. It had nothing to do with her attitude however, but everything to do with how she dressed. She was quickly given the nickname 'Duchess.'

On her typical walk to the Y saloon she would often be wearing her Roberto Cavalli Maroshi Punto knit sheath dress, her Christine Moore Kim – Panama leather yellow sun hat, and her black Brunello Cucinelli diamond dust studded ostrich slip-on shoes. She was quite a sight to the locals and truckers who passed her along highway 247. She always sat at the same seat in the saloon as if owned it, and gave everyone an air of defiant superiority. When the regulars would stream in on Friday nights to watch ESPN sports, they would deliberately make the effort to walk by her seat and exclaim: 'How's it going today, Duchess?' Ruby would simply give a silent nod and continue drinking her vodka and orange juice.

2

For the past ten months now Ruby has been stone-cold sober. She attended a local group of Alcoholics Anonymous in the backroom of the Chemehuevi Community Center five blocks away. The motel owner was worried about her and finally talked her into going with him to the group. Her initial motivation for going was to get him off her back, but then she started looking forward to the everyday meetings, because it gave her something to do, something to focus on. She really had no choice however. This place out in the middle of the desert was her last stand. One more drink would probably be her last, because she would be dead.

The Roach and its varied and colorful collection of broken souls was all that was left to Ruby's life. Pathetic. How goddamn pathetic, she thought. She took the last swallow of her now warm soda when someone tapped on her window, startling her away from her secret thoughts. She lowered the window while fidgeting with the cigarette lighter.

"Howdy-do, Ruby. Chillin' out are ya?"

Ruby looked up at the man who intruded on her thoughts. Pete Roach was an eighty-something, skinny black guy, with closely cropped snow white hair. His clothes looked like they were leftovers from the seventies: white leather shoes, green leisure pants and a shirt straight off the racks of Kmart. Pete was a thirty-year Navy man, recovering alcoholic, with tightly held traditional values. He was always laughing or smiling and optimistic about everything. A day barely went by without a joke or clever saying from the man. He walked with a cane now after a bad fall two years ago. The man perpetually smelled of tobacco, sweat and Old Spice.

"Hey, ya gonna just sit there or are ya gonna open up the other door and share some of that chilly air," Pete said with a very grave expression and voice to match. Now what does he want, thought Ruby, as she pushed the unlock switch. Pete settled into the passenger side and started rubbing his hand over the nice dashboard.

"You sound like you have something important to say," said Ruby.

"I do in fact," said Pete, as he continued rubbing his hand over the nice dash area, that had enough buttons, gadgets and lights to make it seem like the cockpit of a small aircraft.

"You know, Ruby, this is quite the beautiful car. One could stay in it all the time without ever wanting to leave." Ruby just rolled her eyes.

"The point, Pete. The goddamn point! You have something to say, so just say it." Pete folded his hands around the top of his cane that rested between his legs. He looked at Ruby with a seriousness she had never seen before until now.

"It's about Laila."

"Oh, what's up with the queen bitch now?"

"I wish you wouldn't talk about her like that Ruby, she really does mean well, ya know."

Ruby never liked the woman since the first day they met. Laila Chaudry hailed from the Punjabi district of Northern Pakistan. She was the motels cook who ran the café with an iron fist. At times she reminded Ruby of the soup Nazi character on the Seinfeld TV show. Rumors abounded among the motel residents and town people on why she came here twenty-five years ago when Pete bought the place. Ruby heard that she was running from the law in Pakistan for dark deeds, but the reason is almost as tightly held as a state secret by Pete.

When confronted about the reason for all the secrecy, Laila would give the person a high and mighty look, stick her chin outwards, grunt and turn away. The redeeming quality about the woman was that she was a damn good cook. Her weekly special of a simple burger and fries with homemade hot pepper, mango chutney was out of this world.

Pete paused to gather his thoughts again.

"Laila found out that she has two elderly aunts living in Bakersfield, and they want her to come and live with them and help with things."

"Good. So what's stopping her?"

"It's a matter of transportation."

"So, she's too good to take the Greyhound bus like everyone else?"

"I was thinking you might want to give her your car."

"What the hell. Why on earth would I ever do that," screamed Ruby.

"Well Ruby, it's like this. My old Ford pickup wouldn't make it beyond a hundred miles because of all the work it needs. And your driver's license was revoked for life. You really have no need of this car no more. It's part of your past. You need to let it go and start healing your emotional scars. Driving down here from Denver like you did was pretty darn risky. California would have throw'd your butt in jail for a long time while driving revoked."

"That may be so Pete, but what's in it for me," said Ruby, nearly shouting.

"Now keep it down Ruby. I'm not deaf. It's all about redemption, Ruby. Redemption ain't worth squat unless someone besides yourself benefits. It's all part of recovery from your former life. Payback if you will. And what I'm really saying is giving back something that is important to you, something you're attached to."

Ruby pounded the steering wheel with both fists and spoke directly and slowly at Pete.

"But why now, why her of all people?"

"Laila is a very proud woman. She needs the recognition that she made something of herself, that she accomplished something important these last twenty-five years, without the approval or help from a husband. Plus, she needs this nice ride to help out her elderly aunts. Imagine this, Ruby. Picture in your mind Laila driving up to her aunt's place in your shiny SUV and announcing her retirement from a successful business."

Ruby frowned and said, "Okay, go on…"

"See, that kind of thing is really important to her people and it would cast her in a favorable light with her family. And furthermore, it would make her happy as a clam. She deserves this after what her husband did to her twenty-five years ago."

"So what happened with that?"

"When she was a young married woman she announced to her husband that she had signed up for college to get a business degree. Since hubby was a very strict Muslim he wanted nothing of it, so he beat her and threw her out on the street. Somehow she made it here from Chicago. She deserves a break as much as you deserve redemption."

"I see," said Ruby as she gave Pete a thousand-yard stare.

"All I ask Ruby, is that you sleep on it tonight."

"If she leaves who will run the café?"

"I was thinking that would be a good job for you – my new manager. It would give you something to do, to focus on while you're sorting out your past. And it would bring some new, fresh blood to the place. Free room and board comes with the position." Ruby's jaw slightly dropped open as she turned and stared at Pete.

3

Ruby opened the door to her room and immediately thanked her lucky stars she left the A/C running. It was your typical basic room at your typical run-down motel out in the middle of the desert. There was a queen size bed in the middle of the room with a coffee table on one side and a tall lamp on the other.

The bathroom was off to the right of the door. The cheap, ugly wallpaper of green and blue foliage was stained brown in a few spots and peeling near the ceiling. A picture of Yosemite Falls hung above the bed. Some might consider this a tasteless joke in a place like this. Over in the corner, to the left of the door, was a small desk and chair with a black rotary dial phone that no longer worked.

She closed the door, threw her empty soda can in the waste basket, and then walked over to the window and stared out into the twilight. As she watched the burnt-orange colors fade behind the mountains off in the distance, she couldn't help but think of all the desperate people that had come through this place in the past twenty-five years.

As she stared intensely outside, she thought about what Pete said about redemption. She also thought about Laila being beaten and tossed out of her home for the simple desire of wanting an education. She thought about her own circumstances and how she single-handedly destroyed her wonderful life, a life that any other woman would have envied. Ruby was feeling quite defeated this evening and the old desire for a vodka tonic made her lick her lips.

Looking out the window and watching the last vestiges of color disappeared behind the mountains, something suddenly hit the window with a muffled crack. Ruby stepped back and noticed the wind had come up out of nowhere and was blowing quite hard now. Bits of sand hit the window again. The tall and formidable Joshua trees in the distance looked like slow moving *things* in the darkness.

Turning and walking over to her bed she suddenly stopped dead in her tracks. The hairs in her ears bristled and goosebumps appeared all up and down on both arms. She immediately crossed her arms, shivered, turned full circle, and listened intently. What is that, she thought?

A strange sound seemed to be coming from outside. Ruby walked back to the window and opened it fully, letting in a strong blast of hot air. She listened with a resolute manner, craning her neck in such an odd way, it almost hurt. The sound was magnified greatly with the window open.

At first it sounded like whistling, then small mournful barks that became a chorus. It then evolved into a low-pitched roar, and then suddenly ending in four distant booms. These sounds were beautiful in their own way, like murmuring angel voices.

Ruby stood at the open window awhile longer, completely transfixed by the strange sounds coming off the desert. She finally closed the window. She immediately went over to her bed and lay down, curled in a fetal position, still staring at the window. She couldn't shake the feeling that among those strange sounds, there were a murmuring of many voices rising and falling.

She knew she wasn't dying but nevertheless her life flashed before her in all of its miserable majesty. That gnawing hunger for just one drink finally went away and was replaced by a euphoric, light-headedness. The sounds from outside still haunted her to the core of her being. The sounds seemed to be telling her something but she was clueless as to what it was. The only way Ruby could describe it was as if someone or something had spoken to her from a great distance, attempting to reveal an important message.

The sounds were eerily beautiful and put her immediately at peace. She knew exactly what she needed to do and there was no turning back from that decision. Was there a Supreme Being after all, and was this the way It communicated with us, thought Ruby? She finally got tired of thinking about it close to 3 am, undressed and pulled the bed sheet over herself, and waited for sleep to come.

The next morning was still uncomfortably warm. Ruby stood outside her room and gazed out into the expanse of the desert, tilted her head to the left, and then tried to listen for that strange music she heard last night. Nothing. Nothing other than the wind and sounds coming from the parking lot of the Lucerne Market & Deli five blocks away. She felt slightly enervated this morning and the motel environs didn't seem as drab and hellish as before.

She noticed a new beauty to the forlorn desert before her. As she looked over at her shiny, silver SUV, it seemed odd and out-of-place to her. It looked alien, from another time and place. It was as if it didn't belong to her. Then suddenly a tumbleweed streaked across the parking lot giving her a start. It bolted her from her reverie. She closed the door to her room and pressed a small cigar box close to her side, and began walking towards the café for breakfast.

Describing the Roach Motel & Café as broken down was probably too generous. The place was around sixty years old and memories of better times were all but forgotten. The paint was peeling on just about every surface of the motel buildings. The once green exterior with deep and bright forest trim was now a faded olive drab. The porch that led to the café was horribly blistered and worn from years of sun, wind and sand. The deck chairs were rickety and held together with layers of duct tape.

As Ruby opened the café door aromas of hot coffee and bacon assaulted her senses. Today's breakfast special was her favorite: grits, bacon and a sunny side up egg. However, the coffee was always scorched beyond recognition but at least it was hot.

The inside of the café still pretty much looked like it did decades ago, even the coke machine, milkshake mixer and cold case had never made it beyond the 1950's. The walls were covered with a yellow and white floral wallpaper that was now faded almost beyond recognition. The place only seated fifteen but was never crowded. Most of the customers were motel residents with the occasional traveler stopping in for a quick lunch, or just coffee, pie and directions to the next major town.

The brindle colored linoleum floor was faded and cracked, and the six tables always sat unevenly with wads of cardboard underneath one or more legs. A black and gold crushed velvet tapestry of Elvis hung on the far wall, above a rickety wood table that had two-year old magazines and pop fiction books piled high. This was the official library for the motel guests.

There were only three people in the café this morning. Laila was hard at work at the grill while Pete sat at the counter slurping a big cup of coffee. He had his regular stack of sour dough toast smothered with butter and grape jelly – his favorite breakfast. At the other end of the counter sat Evan Caulfield.

Ruby had formed an opinion of him early on and thought he was a know-it-all as well as a complete ass. She always avoided sitting near him because of his serial potty mouth – not just an occasional shit, damn or bastard, but every other word in a normal conversation was foul. The man seemed to have a limited vocabulary even though he was always trying to convince others how smart he was, especially when he threw in a couple of really big words.

Evan was an extremely bitter and lonely, middle-aged, balding man. Dressed all in black, coffee cup in one hand, cigarette in the other, wearing sun glasses, he sat there staring out of the big, dirty picture window. His cleanly shaved face was always void of any emotion, and appeared not to be connected with anyone else in the room.

Ruby had heard from Pete that Caulfield checked in for one night five years ago. An extremely young lady checked in that same night. It seemed to be love at first sight; they talked and danced the night away at the Y Saloon. The next morning the young lady left for Los Angeles, saying she needed to pack a few things and would be right back. She never was seen or heard from again. Caulfield has waited diligently every day, staring out that window, hoping for her return.

Ruby made her way to the seat next to Pete and plopped herself down and put the small cigar box off to the side.

"Well good morning, Ruby."

"Morning."

Pete looked at her up and down and shook his head.

"My, oh my. White top, blue jeans and tennis shoes. Dressing down are we?"

Ruby ignored Pete's comment. Then Laila came over and poured Ruby a steaming cup of coffee.

"Will you be having the special?"

"Yes I will," said Ruby, as she dumped lots of cream and sugar into her coffee and gave it a quick stir. She watched Laila a moment doing her usual routine at the grilling station. Ruby thought it was remarkable how organized and efficient this woman was behind the counter.

"There's something about you this morning, Ruby, something different. It seems like you're walking on a cloud or something," said Pete, as he gazed at her intently. He looked at the cigar box she had brought with her.

"Have you given anymore thought to what we talked about last night?" added Pete.

"I did," said Ruby, as she watched Laila put her breakfast plate before her. She drizzled maple syrup all over the grits, bacon and egg. Pete got her to try it this way and ended up liking it. He told her that growing up in Alabama as a young boy his mother served it this way and called it breakfast grits. Pete looked on approvingly as Ruby took a couple of mouthfuls, closed her eyes and savored the delicious breakfast.

Ruby finally put her spoon down and gave Laila a firm look. She then took from the small cigar box a piece of paper and lay it on the counter.

"Pete here told me everything – even how your husband beat you and tossed you out of your own home."

Laila frowned quite deeply and looked straight at Pete.

"But why? I thought that conversation we had many years ago was confidential."

Pete hurriedly took a big slurp of his coffee while looking at Ruby.

"I think Ruby has some good news for you. I just hope so."

On that note Ruby handed the piece of paper to Laila. She looked at it and looked at Ruby. She looked at it again, and then back at Ruby.

"What is this about?"

"That is the pink slip to my car and as you can see, I have already signed it over to you."

"But why?"

"Listen to me, Laila. Pete told me your story. And I did a lot of soul searching last night. If there's anyone who deserves my car it's you. Anyway, as you probably already know my story, that car parked outside this past year represents my old life, and I can't even drive it legally anymore."

Ruby looked over at Pete, nodded and continued.

"You're not the only one getting something here, Laila. I'm getting my self-esteem back. I'm getting some of that old-fashioned redemption Pete spoke to me about last night, and it feels pretty good right about now. It's the right thing to do. Last night I had a moment. And what I mean by that, is my life flashed before me after I heard some strange music coming from the desert. I realized this time was different. had to finally cut the cord to my past and start living in the present each day. I can't go back again. If I do, I'll probably end up drinking myself to death. Also, I am giving you these trinkets of mine. Inside this cigar box is a matching diamond bracelet, ear rings and necklace. They are worth around $130,000. A certificate of authentication is included. I know you don't wear jewelry but you can sell them and use the money for your retirement. I'll have Pete here lock them up in the motel safe until you're ready to leave. In the next couple of days I'll walk into town and get a notarized letter that I gave you the stones as a gift."

Laila put the pink slip down and then rushed around from behind the counter and gave Ruby a big bear hug, and both women immediately started crying.

"You have made me so happy, Ruby. Now I can retire properly and show my aunties just how successful I have been. I can't wait to see their faces when I drive up in that shiny, silver SUV."

Laila then quickly composed herself, dried her eyes with a napkin and then finished refilling coffee for Evan at the end of the counter. She came back where Ruby and Pete sat.

"So Pete, who is going to run the café when I leave?" Pete pointed his finger at Ruby.

"Meet your successor."

Laila looked a bit startled at first, but then started chattering about all the necessary things that needed to be done before departing for Bakersfield. Pete looked at Ruby, smiled softly and lightly touched her hand.

"You did the right thing, Ruby. I'm so proud of you."

Evan Caulfield got up from his chair and joined the other three at the end of the counter.

"Couldn't help over-hearing the goddamn story – an amazing fucking story at that. It almost makes you want to cry like a little girl. Let say we all have a drink and celebrate."

Pete gave Evan a hard, unsmiling look.

"This isn't the time or place Evan. Why not go back over there in your corner and finish reading your newspaper."

Evan just threw up his hands and slowly walked back to his corner seat and resumed reading the paper and puffing away on his cigarette.

4

The four weeks were a flurry of activity at the Roach Motel. When Laila wasn't sorting through her personal possessions of twenty-five years, she was diligently teaching Ruby how to run the café; from keeping records of the supplies purchased to customer receipts and how to clean the aging grill station properly.

During this time both women set aside any differences they had and grew to respect each other. After all, it wasn't about them individually but the survival and success of the Roach. Pete would often come into the café to see how the women were getting along. He would sit at the counter, drink his coffee, and smile approvingly at their team work.

When the day finally arrived to say goodbye to Laila, Evan and a few other residents stood with Pete in front of the café to say their farewells. Laila had the SUV packed with her possessions – which really wasn't much at all – but very important possessions to say the least.

After giving Pete a long tearful hug and a simply wave to the others, she climbed into the SUV and proceeded out of the parking lot. As she stopped before turning onto highway 247, Ruby was standing at the corner near what was left of a now useless phone booth.

Both women silently looked at each other for a moment. Time seemed to have stopped and eternity lay before them like a colorful, spinning mosaic that never stops – always in motion, grinding away towards an unknown future. Ruby put both palms together and raised them above her head and gave Laila the biggest, precious smile she could muster.

Laila bit her trembling lower lip and tears flowed down her cheeks. As the SUV disappeared and became a tiny dot on the horizon, Ruby realized that the last link to her former life and former ways was now gone forever. She could now move forward and start living instead of merely surviving.

As Ruby walked back to join the others still standing in front of the café, Evan blurted out in his usual, nasty half-ass manner.

"What in the fucking hell was that all about?"

Pete looked over at Ruby who was trying to ignore Evan and said:

"Where Laila comes from that thing Ruby did just now is a sign of great respect and farewell to an elder."

"But Laila is obviously younger than Ruby," said Evan.

"Yes. Yes she is, isn't she," said Pete as he gave Ruby a big, almost comical wink.

A month later in the late evening Ruby, Pete and Evan were sitting at the counter having coffee and peach pie. The conversation soon drifted to Laila and how she was doing in her new home.

"Feels kind of quiet and lonely around here without the old gal bustling about," said Pete.

"I'm not missing her one bit," blurted Evan. "The bitch used to order me about like I was some scumbag or something. No respect whatsoever."

Ruby looked hard at Evan.

"If you want respect, well sometimes you have to give a little first."

Evan straightened up and glared at Ruby. Pete saw what was happening and quickly changed the subject.

"You know Ruby, I've been curious about your experience that night, you know, hearing music and singing from the desert and all that. There's a legend around these parts of people hearing the same thing. Some of the Chemehuevi people over in Needles talk about it often and say it's the voice of the Great Spirit talking to us."

"You can flush all that mystical mumbo-jumbo bull crap down the toilet," said Evan defiantly.

"Oh. Are you an expert on such matters," mumbled Ruby, as she finished the last of her peach cobbler.

"In fact I am, girlee. What you described is the *singing sands phenomena*. Geologists have written quite extensively on the matter. Let me try to explain it so that pretty little head of yours can understand it. Singing, whistling or barking sand is sand that produces sound. You see, certain conditions have to come together to create the singing sand effect. The sand grains have to be circular and between 0.1 and 0.5 millimeters in diameter. The sand has to contain silica. The sand needs to be at a certain humidity."

Ruby and Pete sat there not quite knowing how to respond while Evan continued talking.

"There are several theories about the singing sands and how that works. It has been proposed that the sound frequency is controlled by the shear rate. Some geologists have suggested that the frequency of vibration is related to the thickness of the dry surface layer of sand.

The sound waves bounce back and forth between the surface of the dune and surface of the moist layer, creating a resonance that increases the sound's volume. The noise may be generated by friction between the grains or by the compression of air between them. Sometimes it gives off a booming or roaring sound. See, that's what you heard that night. Not some mystical, crazy god talking to you."

"You sound pretty damn sure of yourself, don't you", said Pete, while winking at Ruby.

"It's all about logic, rational thinking and scientific evidence", declared Evan.

"I don't think it's a bad thing if you read something mystical into that, as long as it helps you on your way. I hate it when people get so full of themselves, and start dividing up the natural world into such black and white terms. Sometimes we need a little mystery to get through this thing we call life, just saying," said Pete, as he raised both hands up. He looked over at Ruby who was playing with the crumbs on her plate with her fork.

"What do you think, Ruby? Was it the Great Spirit talking or just particles of sand rubbing up against each other, all cozy like," said Pete.

Ruby put down her fork, took a napkin and wiped her mouth ever so delicately, while staring at Evan. She finally spoke after a long pause.

"To begin with Evan, I don't even understand what you said. As far as I'm concerned your theory is just plain crap because it's coming from you. I don't trust anything you say anymore on any subject. Maybe if a real scientist was here and explained it in such a way for me to understand, I just may give him the time of day. What I heard that night was incredible and beyond words. It changed me somehow and that's all I care about. I don't care about the mechanics behind such an event. I may not necessarily believe in a Great Spirit, but then again neither can I accept a world where everything is rationally explained and button-holed to support some theory. There has to be some mystery in life. I need that mystery because it gives me hope for something better. That music from the desert that night gave me the strength to move forward, and I'm not about to question that – not at this point anyway."

Evan stood up from the counter, downed the last bit of coffee and flippantly declared:

"You just keep believing that fuckin' bullshit and see where it gets you. I'm tired of arguing with women who think they know so much about everything. I'm tired. I'm going to bed."

Ruby and Pete watched Evan walk out of the café, slamming the screen door.

5

The next morning was already getting quite warm – it was predicted to be a scorcher today. Pete was waiting for Ruby at the café when she arrived. He had a bag lunch and two bottles of iced cold coca cola waiting for both of them on the counter. Ruby walked into the café, looked at Pete and then at the lunch sacks and cokes.

"What's this? Going on a picnic, Pete?"

"No. Actually we both are. We're driving over to the big rock, Monument Rock, this morning. It only takes five minutes by car."

"Oh. What's the occasion?" said Ruby.

"I was thinking about that experience you talked about to Evan and me yesterday. I think it's time I took you on a visit to one of the strangest places on the West coast. I think you're ready for it, to understand it, to absorb the significance of the place. I also have a story to tell you while we're there having brunch. It's a story passed down to me from a Chemehuevi elder some years back, when I needed to learn a certain lesson. So let's say we get started."

"What about the café? We just can't walk away. Someone might stop by."

"We won't be gone that long, anyway, if someone wants an early morning pie and coffee they can go to the deli at the Lucerne market," said Pete.

The short drive to Monument Rock was done in silence, except for the sputtering and rattling of Pete's old 1966 Ford pickup. As Pete pulled his pickup to within twenty feet of the rock, Ruby's face changed expression and her mouth dropped wide open. Pete looked over at her with that big toothy smile. This was no ordinary rock. It stood at seven stories high and was around six-thousand square feet in diameter.

Monument Rock, as it was called by the locals, was the biggest free-standing boulder on the West coast of the United States. They got out of the truck, and Pete grabbed Ruby's hand and walked her around the entire base, while telling her about the popular tales that had grown up around it. Some believable and others not so much. He stated that the rock had become a magnet for New Ager's and UFO cultists.

"This looks like a good place to sit and talk. Why don't you get us the cokes, blanket, lunch bags, and I'll tell you my story."

Ruby came back and spread the blanket, all the while looking for any snakes, then helped Pete sit down.

"I feel like a child on a picnic today," blurted Ruby. She was hungry and immediately took out the fried egg, cheese and ham sandwich that Pete had prepared. It was still slightly warm and smeared with mustard and mayo. After they both took a couple of bites and had a drink of soda Pete started his story.

"This story supposedly took place just outside what we know today as San Bernardino around 1895. The Chemehuevi elder called it the '*Story of the Twenty Dollar Boy.*'"
Pete took a long deep breath and paused a bit, while he gazed up at Monument Rock.

"Please listen carefully," said Pete.

Tomas was happy. Today was his 12th birthday. His father woke him early to take him on his first hunt. When the two arrived at their destination after several hours walking, they were met by three white men. The taller one looked at the boy up and down, scratched his chin, and then said to the father: 'He will do nicely. He has potential.' The man then thrust a twenty-dollar bill into the father's hand. The father greedily put it away in his waist pouch.

He gave his boy one final look and walked away. Tomas was greatly confused. He wanted to run after his father but the taller white man grabbed him quickly with an iron grip. Tomas struggled with all his might but the grip was impossible to break. He screamed and begged for his father to come back.

Tomas suffered greatly under the care of these three men. He soon found out that he had been sold into indentured servitude to pay off his father's gambling and drinking debts. But Tomas grew strong in body due to all the hard work while his hatred for his father grew ever stronger. This hatred kept him going year after year, even when he wanted to give up and die.

One day shortly after Tomas turned 16, his Master released him from his indentured servitude. He was finally free. Tomas' first thought and mission in life was to find his father and kill him. For the next two years Tomas looked high and low. He even visited his old home but his family had long since moved on. He worked odd jobs on the railroad and gained a reputation as a strong, hard worker who could be depended upon.

Then one day outside a general store he saw a man who looked many years beyond his age. The man had all the appearances of someone who drank heavily. Tomas had seen it before, and it always disgusted him how anyone could let themselves be taken over by liquor. The man was obviously blind, feeble and had a pair of crutches next to him on the steps. The old man senses Tomas' presence and asked him if he could spare a quarter.

Tomas asked the man how he let himself get into such condition. The man quickly told him his story in hopes of getting a quarter in return. He told Tomas that years ago he drank heavily and ran up a big gambling debt with three white men. When it was time to pay his debt he didn't have the money. He ended up selling his only son into indentured servitude to pay off the debt. Soon afterwards his wife took his two daughters and abandoned him. He became sorry for what he did and tried to find his son but failed. He soon drank himself into a deep sleep every night for the next number of years.

Tomas listened carefully to the old man's story and knew that he finally found his father. The murderous rage he had kept bottled up for all those years left him instantly, after seeing what his father had become. The man asked again for a quarter. Tomas looked up into the sky for a moment and then gave his father four quarters – his week's wages – then quickly departing the area, without saying anything or looking back. A deep sigh of relief came over Tomas and he knew that he could live his life now, unhindered from his past.

"That's a sad story. But I'm glad the boy was able to move on with his life," said Ruby.

"It's a story about redemption, Ruby. No matter what others have done to you, you need to forgive and forget and move on. Just like when all your friends and family abandoned you, when you needed them the most, you need to forgive them for what they did. After all, you did something pretty horrible yourself by running down and crippling that person in the cross walk while driving drunk."

"Why are you so wise, Pete?"

Pete just gave her that big comical wink of his and said they best be getting back to the café to wait on customers.

6

Life continued as usual at the Roach Motel & Café for the next year. Ruby busied herself learning all the ins and outs of running a café and making some small improvements here and there. Everyone, including Ruby, ended up missing Laila and her abrupt ways more than they would ever admit. Ruby started having conversations with Pete on putting some money into the place and making it more appealing to the public. Pete was always resistant to this idea however.

Ruby found out that Pete was sitting on a sizable amount of money, lottery winnings from years ago, and couldn't understand why he was so stingy when it came to dipping into the fund for any reason. She finally let it go and put her nose to the grindstone. It was about this time that everybody started noticing different and strange behaviors from Evan Caulfield. What raised the red flag however was his self-secluding in his room for the past two weeks.

He stopped eating and hanging out at the café. The only time he was seen was when he walked to the Lucerne Market every day at noon to pick up whatever was in his grocery bag. Even when approached he was reluctant to say anything, kept his head down and just passed by the person speaking. Residents were missing his daily belligerent tirades about politics and social life in general.

Today was different. It was already 6:45 pm and nobody had seen him since noon yesterday. When Pete got wind of this he became worried. He asked Ruby to come with him to Evan's room and find out just what was going on. With pass key in hand Pete and Ruby stood at his door. Pete started off with a gentle knock with no response. He then knocked louder and louder until he was banging on the door.

"How can anyone sleep with all that banging," declared Ruby.

Pete finally got the key to work and slowly opened the door, softly calling Evan's name. Ruby and Pete stood aghast at what they saw. Evan lay across the bed on his back, completely nude, still clutching an empty bottle of 30-year old single malt scotch. There was a pool of vomit next to his face. It was all too clear he had choked to death on his own vomit. Ruby walked over and pulled the bottle from his hand.

"What a waste of good liquor."

Pete looked at Evan's prostrate body and said rather quietly, mostly a whisper:

"Some of us are just sicker than others."

"From the look of his vomit he probably died within the past couple of hours or so. There's no smell yet," exclaimed Ruby.

Ruby visibly shuddered as she took in the whole scene like a coroner on the job. The room was heavily cluttered with candy wrappers, half eaten take-out boxes of food, vodka bottles, orange juice cartons, and newspapers. The place was a complete pigsty. No wonder he refused to let the cleaning girl in to do her weekly rounds lately. Ruby thought to herself: this could have been me. She shuddered again.

"What brought him to this end do you think," asked Ruby, as she gazed at Pete.

"All I really know about the man is what he told me a few months after arriving here. He was a math instructor at an all-girls academy in Los Angeles. A very prestigious one at that. He was fired for allegedly having sex with one of his students, even though he bitterly denied it. It seems he finally gave up on everything, including himself."

"I'll go back to the office and call the sheriff and tell him what happened," said Ruby.

Pete slowly walked over to the window and stared out into the twilight. As he watched the burnt-orange colors fade behind the mountains off in the distance, he couldn't help but think about all the desperate people that came through his place in the past twenty-five years. This was the first time however that someone passed on here. He turned and looked down upon the frozen expression of hopelessness on Evan's face. He spoke aloud but ever so softly and gently:

"You never once gave yourself a chance at redemption and to move on with your life. How sad, my friend. How very sad indeed. What a wasted life." A big tear trickled down Pete's wrinkled, leathery face as he let out a tremendous sigh.

Ruby came back and told Pete that the sheriff's deputy would be here within the next fifteen minutes, and no one is not to touch anything in the room. Ruby moved over next to Pete and asked him if he was alright. Pete shook his head side-to-side.

"No, I'm not alright. It's always a shock to see human life wasted in this manner. I really thought that one day I could help Evan make his way out of the big black, ugly pit he dug for himself. But in the end if you lose hope you lose everything, and there's nothing nobody else can do about it, but just watch and wait." Ruby grabbed Pete and gave him a big, long hug and softly whispered in his ear.

"It's sad about Evan, I know. But just think about the impact that your kindness and wisdom had on other people."
She put him at arms-length and stared intently at him.

"You're looking at one of them now."

As the San Bernardino county Sheriff's car pulled into the parking lot with its light bar flickering, Pete went out to meet the deputy and show him to Evan's room. Ruby went over to the café to inform any residents what had happened, and wait for the deputy to do his job. An hour later as she was pouring coffee and passing out the last of the apple cobbler, an ambulance from San Bernardino arrived to take the body away. As the ambulance loaded up its cargo and drove away Pete and the deputy came into the café.

"Ruby, the deputy needs a statement from you also, just as a formality."
Ruby and the deputy talked for about twenty minutes while the other residents hung on every word being said. This was a big thing for them. Stuff like this rarely happens in Lucerne Valley. After the deputy had left they couldn't get enough details from Ruby to satisfy their morbid curiosity.

The death of Evan Caulfield became the talk of the small town for quite some time afterwards. Those who knew him at the Y Saloon argued about whether his death was simply an accident due to over drinking or a planned suicide. A few of the regulars even indulged themselves in some minor conspiracy theories based on things Evan had said during his drunken dialogues, and never looking at the tragic reality of his life inside a bottle.

Eventually the scuttlebutt subsided and most everyone in town forgot that Evan Caulfield even existed. Pete was one of the few that didn't stop remembering him. He saved Evan's sunglasses and positioned them on top of the filing cabinet in the office, as a constant reminder of one that wasn't able to be helped. Pete referred to it as a sad monument of an unredeemed and wasted life.

7

After the whole Evan Caulfield incident, Ruby doubled down and continued her sobriety and kept attending A.A. meetings at the Chemehuevi Community Center. She became good friends with the director of the center and he agreed to become her sponsor. Souza Maynard, a full-blooded Chemehuevi, was not only the director of the center, but he was the unofficial mayor of Lucerne Valley. He wasn't a real mayor, however; nor was he elected by the people; it was an appointed figurehead position, that reported directly to the San Bernardino County Board of Supervisors.

Souza was a short, barrel-chested man in his mid-forties who was soft spoken with measured speech. His short black hair was always plastered down with Brill Crème. He wore snake skin boots, blue denim jeans and native print shirts with metal snaps. He also wore a white cowboy hat with an eagle feather in the band.

He looked like every other Chemehuevi man in town. There was one big difference though. Souza had graduated from UCLA with a master's degree in cultural anthropology. He was smart as a whip and could easily win an argument with anybody, especially white folks, when the subject of religion and politics arose. He was also respected.

Early on Souza had decided not to pursue a doctorate degree and came back to Lucerne Valley, where he was born and raised, and went to work in the family business. His mother Mirabella with his two older siblings, brother Joe and sister Susie, owned and managed a heavy equipment sales & rental company. They had over forty-five employees that offered its services all over San Bernardino county. Souza was an iconic figure around town who was often seen driving his souped-up, 1978 copper-colored El Camino, with red flame stripes on the sides.

The Chemehuevi Community Center became a big part of Ruby's life. She got to know many of the folks there and made several friends. She was amazed at the diversity of beliefs among the Chemehuevi people. Some were Mormon, some Christian and a very few, like Souza, were adherents of the Native American Peyote Church. She was only one of two non-natives that actively participated in the centers activities – Pete being the other one.

Souza became a great help and emotional support to Ruby. She found that he was much wiser than his biological years. In fact, she came to suspect that he was possibly the reincarnation of a great warrior or shaman – but that was just silly fantasy and day-dreaming on her part, when she was bored. He often told Ruby that Great Spirit had great things in store for her. She just had to keep reminding herself of that on a daily basis. With that kind of support from Souza, Ruby would find her way out of the occasional negative funk and progress onward.

Souza taught Ruby about Chemehuevi spirituality, how to honor the earth and its diversity of elements and to respect all life. Ruby absorbed all this like a dry sponge dipped in water. She felt young and alive and thirsting after new knowledge for the first time in many, many years.

She learned that the Chemehuevi, part of the Southern Paiute peoples, believe that supernatural power resides in all living things and in many non-animate objects found in nature, as well as in the sun, moon, stars, wind, and so on. Persons are free to establish a relationship with *objects of power*, but only doctors or shamans possess enough of it to aid in healing.

Their powers come unsought through dreams and visions, or they could be sought by going to certain sacred places, like Monument Rock. Ordinary persons rarely speak of their alleged powers, although the community might know if they had special powers for, let say, large game animals, wolves, snakes or birds.

Ruby also was taught that special classes of spirits, like water babies, dwarfs and changeable beings reside at various places. Encounters with these were considered dangerous. However, today elderly people and some younger persons believe in these spirits and in the power of living things and the earth. What is strangely complex and rich about the Chemehuevi belief system is that it can be tightly intertwined with Mormon and Christian beliefs.

Ruby greatly admired Souza. He not only taught her about living the clean and sober life but taught her many practical things as well. He drove her into the desert and taught her how to shoot a 30.06 rifle and kill a Mojave green rattler at fifty yards. He also taught her how to skin and clean the thing and make a rather tasty stir-fry.

He also taught her about needless killing, like sport hunting, that was morally repugnant to all life. When Ruby had asked him if he went on ritualistic hunts, like in the old days, he simply laughed at her. He said with the great burger and fries at the Roach Motel, killing animals for sustenance basically becomes needless these days.

During the winter, on several occasions, Souza drove Ruby and Pete out into the desert around midnight, and would point out the various stars, constellations and planets. Souza's knowledge of the heavens was truly remarkable. It was during these times when Ruby found out just how close Pete and Souza were. They were best friends that went back twenty-five years. One day when Souza was eighteen, just before leaving for college, some drunk white guys cornered him near the Y Saloon and were going to do him great bodily harm. Pete happened to come by and ran them off with his shot gun. The friendship flourished after that.

8

A year had already gone by since the passing of Evan Caulfield and there were definite changes on the horizon. Ruby sat down with Pete to discuss the work load at the motel. Bridgette Cummings, who lived in town and worked full-time as the motel's maid, decided to quit and move to Los Angeles. She got the opportunity to work at one of the big hotels, with a great wage and benefit package. Everyone was sad to see her go but wished her the best of luck.

With Bridgette leaving and Pete getting up there in years – he just turned eighty-eight – this put a strain on them. Ruby couldn't do everything. She was no spring chicken herself. She felt every bit of her sixty-five years. Pete readily agreed that help was needed. Doris Palatino, who had been living at the motel for several weeks now, agreed to become part of the staff.

Doris was forty years old and just a smidgeon under five-foot-five. She was swarthy of complexion with short black hair and deep, penetrating brown eyes. Her parents hailed from Sicily and came to America as immigrants. Her father was an importer of fine Sicilian furniture and rugs. Her mother was a traditional stay-at-home mom, who raised Doris and her older brother Francis and her younger sister Mary.

When Doris was twenty, she chased her boyfriend into the street and tried to shoot him with his own gun, after nearly two years of his cheating, physical and emotional abuse. She was charged with attempted murder and spent the next ten years incarcerated in a California correctional facility for women. While in prison she got her high school diploma and an associate of applied science degree in small appliance repair.

For the last eight year's she lived in Los Angeles and worked as a night auditor at a hotel. She hated the big city and all that it represented. And there were also too many memories. When her parole came to an end she found her way to the Roach Motel to forget about her past like everyone else, and try to find her way forward in life.

Pete and Ruby offered her free room and board plus a very small monthly stipend. Not only would she be the motels maid but also use Pete's truck to drive into town and pick up supplies, among other errands. Doris agreed without hesitation. It seemed like a good fit because Ruby liked Doris.

She was easy to talk too and often in the past two weeks, would sit outside the Café late at night, smoke cigarettes and talk about their lives and common things they shared. And the best part of the deal was that Doris was extraordinarily handy at fixing things. Three days after arriving at the motel, she got under the hood of Pete's truck and made it purr like a kitten. Pete was beside himself with joy and amazement.

As Pete significantly slowed down, Ruby and Doris took over nearly all the daily operations of the motel. He spent more time just sitting in the café, nursing a cup of black coffee and talking with folks. He wasn't even able to walk around the property like he used to or even drive his truck into town. If he wanted to see folks in town he would ride along with Doris when she bought supplies. Souza Maynard would give him and Ruby a lift to the Chemehuevi Community Center three times a week for an A.A. meeting.

Slowly Ruby persuaded Pete to loosen up on the purse strings and invest in some needed repairs around the place. She convinced Pete to have the half-broken neon sign taken completely down. A nice wooden four-foot high sign was put up at the entrance to the parking lot. It simply said: *Pete's Place*.

Another change, mostly on Doris' part, was convincing Pete to take down the Elvis tapestry in the café. Several residents applauded this event but it was hard on Pete, because he was a man who didn't like change, especially when it came to his motel. They also stripped off all the old wallpaper and put a fresh coat of paint on the walls.

"I guess the women folk are taking over now," Pete jokingly told others.

It was during this time of intense activity that Pete had Souza Maynard drive him over to San Bernardino, so he could sign some important papers at the Evangelista Family Law Center. Everyone was curious about this but Pete held onto his secret with a vengeance. He would simply smile, wink and say:

"Loose lips sink ships."

Souza knew all about Pete's business at the law center but was bound by Pete's word not to divulge any of the details. Souza did offer that Pete made him administrator of his estate so all his wishes could be carried out. The trust and friendship between the two men was a bond like no other.

In the weeks and months that followed, Pete's expression grew more joyful and content. Since the women were in charge, he stopped worrying about all the little significant details of running a motel. He now considered himself retired again. After thirty-years in the Navy and running the motel these past twenty-five years, he deserved the welcome break from daily responsibilities.

9

The posh Hilltop neighborhood of Denver, Colorado was covered in a canopy of mostly blue skies and fluffy white clouds. The early morning weather report predicted an unusually beautiful Spring day with temperatures in the low seventies. Ruby slowly pulled her cobalt blue BMW out of the driveway. She paused momentarily and stared at her house. It was an English Tudor with three floors, six bedrooms, five bathrooms, a full basement with an entertainment center, and swimming pool. She was so proud of it and wouldn't think twice about inviting people over just for a short tour.

Ruby decided to take the long way into downtown by circling Cranmer Park, which was a twenty-three-acre wonderland in the center of Hilltop. She loved Cranmer. It was always filled with song birds, people walking their dogs, couples jogging, and children playing everywhere. It always filled her with happiness to drive around the park and forget about her busy life just for a few minutes. She stopped at the curbside briefly to watch some dogs frolicking on the greenway, as she slammed down a 375ml bottle of Grey Goose vodka.

She continued driving into downtown towards the Buckhorn Exchange on Osage street, Denver's oldest restaurant, to meet her husband and friends for a nice early supper. But first she had to make a detour, and have a quick chat with Wade Newbegin, one of Denver's most powerful and richest movers and shakers.

Wade's idea was to have Ruby run for mayor of Denver – to become the first woman to hold that position. He had already accomplished all the necessary footwork, including polling, and said she had an excellent chance of winning. Ruby was giving Wade's idea lots of serious thought, and even talked it over with her husband and two sons. She had some good ideas on how to pump up the local economy and bring more business to the city, and create much needed jobs in the process.

She pulled up to the Oxford Hotel and gave the valet her keys. She made her way upstairs to the Cruise Room, an Art Deco style bar known for its martini's. This was the place to be for political and social connections. Denver's elite hung out here like it was their second home. Multi-million dollar deals were made here, as well as political decisions that affected the city and state. Power brokers crawled all over this bar like ants after honey, and had been doing so since the nineteen thirties.

Wade was already sitting at a table going through his notes. Ruby joined him and ordered a vodka Collins. She listened intently to him as he lay out his game plan for her candidacy. She ordered another vodka and told him it just might work. It was time to let a woman run this city. However, she was hesitant about going against the old boy's club. Wade put her mind to rest and said not to worry. He told Ruby she was well liked and respected by everyone, and most importantly, she was a Republican.

Ruby finally agreed on Wade's plan and told him to set things in motion. Wade could hardly contain his enthusiasm, and told her he would set up a press conference for next Thursday morning to announce her candidacy. He vigorously shook her hand, kissed her on the cheek, and gathered up his notes and closed his briefcase. Before leaving however, he gave her a grave look, and asked if she could take it easy on the drinking. After all, it was now a public relations issue for a new campaign. He quickly left the room.

Ruby felt a little miffed at Wade for bringing up her drinking. She knew she could hold her liquor better than the best of them. She immediately started thinking about the prospect of running for mayor and it sent a warm wave of excitement through her. She sat there day dreaming and had a few more vodkas before they cut her off. It seems they were always cutting her off lately and she resented it.

Suddenly it dawned on her she was already twenty minutes late for supper. She needed to get across town in a big hurry. Ruby pulled her nice mink jacket on and headed for the lobby. After tipping the valet she started the fifteen-block drive to the Buckhorn.

At the first stop-light she pulled a 375ml bottle of Grey Goose vodka out of her jacket, and slammed it down like it was water. She pressed the pedal to the floor and took off in a roar, not realizing the light hadn't turned green yet. A young woman was in the crosswalk when Ruby's BMW hit her and flung her over the hood. There was a sickening thud, and people on the sidewalk starting screaming.

Ruby woke up quite abruptly and sat straight up in bed. She was covered with sweat and trembling slightly. She looked around the room and it took her a moment for reality to sink in. She got up, went to the bathroom, and got a glass of water. She then walked over to the window and gazed out into the desert night. She could see the parking lot lights of the Lucerne Market in the distance, creating a weird background against the black sky. She turned away from the window, put the cool glass against her face and closed her eyes.

10

It came out of nowhere and was completely unexpected. To this day the towns people still talk about that horrible Sunday afternoon.

The swirling, bubbling brown and black mass was headed straight for Lucerne Valley like a freight train at high speed with no intention of stopping. People out and about started running for cover inside any building that was open. The wind and sand storm blasted through the town with a deadly, vengeful punch, leaving a path of destruction that hadn't been seen for over sixty years.

The business district that lay at the intersection of highway 247 and 18 looked like a war zone. The China House restaurant sustained the worst damage with one side of the building completely blown in and the roof sagging dangerously. The Lucerne Market, Y Saloon, Carol's Style Shop, Chamber of Commerce, VFW Post, and the library also sustained moderate to heavy damage. There were numerous injuries from flying glass and debris, but thank goodness no one was killed.

The motel wasn't spared from nature's fury. The windows to the café and office were blown in as were a few of the rooms. Siding along the front was laying on the ground. Shingles and other debris littered the parking lot. Ruby was standing in the middle of the parking lot with several residents surveying the damage. She then suddenly thought about Pete. Where was he, she thought, suddenly becoming concerned.

Doris came running from the office wildly flaying her arms, shouting something incoherent. Her face was cut and bleeding as well as her hand. Ruby and the others immediately ran to the motel office. Inside was a complete mess. Almost everything that wasn't bolted down was blown all over the place. The north window had blown in and the large metal filing cabinet had toppled on top of Pete. Doris had managed to move it off him to one side.

Pete lay there on the floor grimacing in pain.

"I think my hip's broke and I can't move my left arm," he murmured.

Ruby sat on the floor next to Pete and told him not to move while she grabbed the phone and dialed 911. She turned to the two male residents standing over them, and with a forceful command voice she blurted out:

"Run into town and get somebody here quick – tell them Pete's hurt bad."

Both men bolted from the office and ran like antelopes across the parking lot, dodging and leaping over debris. Meanwhile the 911 operator told Ruby emergency crews had already been dispatched to Lucerne Valley and should be arriving shortly. Ruby looked at Pete, laying her hand on his chest.

"Stay with me Pete, help is on the way, okay?"

Pete opened his eyes and with his good hand clasped her hand on his chest.

"Don't worry Ruby, I'm not ready to leave just yet." He gave her a big but painful wink.

The next month the residents of Lucerne Valley cleaned up the mess left by the storm and went on with their daily lives. Pete spent a week in the San Bernardino hospital with a broken hip, fractured arm and severe concussion. He then was moved to a rehab center. Doris used Pete's truck and drove Ruby to visit Pete every Wednesday and Sunday for a few hours.

After each visit the two women would stop in at a local Mexican restaurant, have lunch and discuss the future of the motel. Ruby had Pete sign-off several big checks for the repairs and day-to-day operations. Pete's tight-fisted approach to money seemed to disappear and he just signed the checks Ruby gave him without comment. It seemed to Ruby and Doris as if he didn't care anymore.

Pete was the kind of fellow that was independent and always did things for himself. Down deep inside he was probably aware that he could never take care of himself again and be independent. And the thought of moving from rehab to an assisted living home, even for a while, made him quite introspective and gloomy.

He lost his sense of humor, which had always been his best weapon against the world. And then on the forty-fifth day after the accident, Pete passed away in the middle of the night. The staff at the rehab center said he had a very peaceful look on his face, and there didn't seem to be any struggle during his transition.

It was five in the morning when Ruby got the call about Pete's passing. She was completely taken by surprise, because she really thought Pete would come out the other end okay and have a few good years left. She didn't know what to do. Pete was always there for her during the difficult times and he was always like the Rock of Gibralter in this crazy, stupid and mixed-up world.

Ruby dealt with this loss the only way she had learned to deal with life in the past – through a bottle. As soon as the Lucerne Market opened at 6 am, she walked the short distance and bought a bottle of Russian vodka and went back to her room.

Around 8:30 am Souza Maynard showed up at Ruby's door, knocked briefly and then entered. Ruby was sitting on the floor, near her bed and back against the wall. The bottle of vodka was sitting next to her opened. Only a very small amount had been drunk. Ruby had her head buried in her hands and was silently weeping and moaning. She noticed the intrusion and looked up at Souza.

"You here to save me from myself?"

"No Ruby. I'm here to offer some comfort in your time of need. That's all."

Souza sat down on the floor across from Ruby, crossed his legs and put his folded hands in his lap.

"How did you find out I needed help?"

"Joselyn over at the market called me at home right away when you bought the booze. She was concerned that something big had happened and didn't want you to destroy yourself."

"How precious of her."

"She was concerned Ruby. You may not know this but you have lots of people in this town who care about you."

"Pete died this morning! I wasn't expecting it. I wanted him to be around for a few more years."

"That's indeed very sad news, Ruby. I'm going to miss the man a whole lot also. He was unique. He was very human. He gave of himself more than most can ever hope to give. The world is going to be a little bit emptier without him. We need more like him."

"I don't know what to do, Souza."

"You already know what to do, Ruby. It's inside of you. It has always been there. You have turned away and refused to see it, especially now under these circumstances. You have two paths before you. One ends in darkness and death. The other in light and life."

"Are you going to take the bottle away from me?"

"No. Not at all. That's not my job. That's your decision. It always has been. Maybe you can wash your face and dry those tears and come over to the motel café. Others might be worried about you."

Souza leaned forward, put his forehead against Ruby's, put his hand on the back of her neck, and mumbled something strange in his native language. Souza then left Ruby's room and headed to the café for coffee.

When Ruby showed up at the café, Souza had already informed everybody that Pete had passed. Doris was the first one to rush up to Ruby and give her a big hug and a kiss on the cheek.

"Ruby, I think I speak for everyone here. We're so sorry. We know how special Pete was to you. We're here to help you get through this. Just give us a chance. We love you, girl!"

For the next couple of hours, while everyone drank coffee and ate pastries, each person told their favorite story about Pete and how he affected their life. The mood had turned from gloomy to lightness and laughter as people told their stories. It turned out to be a cathartic experience for everyone involved.

11

The sun was just barely peeking over the mountains off in the distance, with a patchwork of orange and pink clouds spread across the horizon. It was slightly cool but not so that one had to bundle up with a heavy jacket. One couldn't have asked for a better day.

Ruby stood on the porch of the motel office with her hiking boots on, blue jeans, a flannel blouse and a light sweater. She clutched the two-quart canister of Pete's ashes close to her chest, as if protecting him from harm.

The package was wrapped in white muslin with a gold cross emblazoned on the side. The funeral home made the assumption that Pete had been of the Christian faith – which he was – but the man had never stepped foot inside a church for nearly sixty years. Pete's last wish was not to have a service of any kind, especially inside a church.

She started the two-mile walk to Monument Rock in a brisk manner. Along the way she made a special effort to notice everything around her: the towering Joshua trees, cactus plants, creosote bushes, a black ground squirrel, a horned lizard perched atop a rock, pinion jays everywhere, squawking and swooping down on her.

Halfway to her destination, Ruby was awarded a special treat of watching a mother jack rabbit with her two babies scurry across the path. The mother stopped, stood high on her haunches, and looked back at Ruby as if saying good morning. At that moment the morning sun burst forth above the horizon like a fiery globe.

She finally arrived at Monument Rock. She sat down on the ground with the package before her. She spoke to it as if Pete was inside and could hear her.

"Well Pete, here we are alone at last. It's going to be tough not having you around anymore to irritate the hell out of me. But I realize it was time for you to move on and start that long journey into the starry night you always spoke about. In many ways you were my hope, my rock, a shoulder to lean upon. You were always there when I needed you the most. You taught me how to take my power back. For this alone I honor you good friend."

Ruby stood up, opened the package, and faced Monument Rock. After a brief pause with her eyes shut, she started sprinkling his ashes around the base of the rock, as she sang his favorite song, *You are my sunshine, My only sunshine.*

When the last of the ashes were sprinkled, she set the empty package down against the base of the rock. At that moment she could have sworn an oath on the bible of getting a big whiff of tobacco, sweat and Old Spice. She turned around several times as if someone were watching her.

And then the tears poured down her face like an open water faucet. She stood there for what seemed like eternity blubbering like a baby. The tears finally stopped. She looked up into the morning sky, and let out with a tremendous sigh.

When Ruby arrived back at the motel it was already 8 am. She stood at the edge of the parking lot surveying the property. She pursed her lips hard and declared in an almost inaudible whisper:

"Things are definitely going to change around here. The first order of business is to start renovations right away, with that big pile of money Pete left me."

She put her hands on her hips and thought of a more appropriate name for her motel – The Singing Sands Motel & Café. With that resolve she marched into the café for breakfast and told everyone about all the new changes that were coming down the pike.

12

Fifteen Years Later

Around noon on a cool December day, a large crowd gathered in the parking lot of the Singing Sands Motel for Ruby's memorial service. For a small town like Lucerne Valley, the crowd was indeed large. Forty-three people came to the service. Most of the town businesses closed temporarily. The only place that stayed open was the 76 gas station on the highway.

Folks said afterward that they couldn't even remember a time when such a crowd gathered together in one spot. Every resident of the motel was present, as were the staff at the Chemehuevi Community Center, the Lucerne Valley Market, the Saloon, and the sheriff's substation.

Souza Maynard and Ruby's youngest son Tommy, walked out of the motel office and stood before the crowd of mourners. Souza raised Ruby's cane over his head with one arm, the same cane that she inherited from Pete years ago. It was a black walnut polished stick with an ivory-like duck head for a handle.

He gazed around at the crowd momentarily, and then he looked to the sky and let loose with a blessing in the Chemehuevi language. Upon finishing he offered the cane to Tommy using both hands, as if he were passing on a sacred chalice. Souza then stepped forward a few steps and said the following:

"We are gathered at this spot today to honor a beloved and departed friend. This spot was chosen specifically because when Ruby first arrived here this is where her car was parked. Three times a week like clockwork she would sit in her car with the windows up, the A/C on high, smoke her cigarettes and listen to her favorite music. She would run the engine for forty-five minutes because she was no longer able to drive. Everybody here knows why so I won't get into that. For one year this spot was her refuge, a fortress if you will. She used this spot as a stepping off point into the next phase of her life. In many ways Ruby was just like the rest of us, leading a life of quiet desperation, but in other ways she rose to achieve a certain level of greatness. A greatness that will be remembered by many whose lives were touched by her generosity and wisdom. Her past was filled with misery and chaos. But in one single evening many years ago her life was profoundly changed by the music of the desert. There is a kind of music that happens in the desert which is known as the Singing Sands. If you live in the desert long enough you may eventually hear it, because the white noise of civilization has been reduced to a negligible amount."

Souza paused momentarily and squinted at the sun which was now directly above the crowd. He continued his speech:

"To some folks, especially the Chemehuevi peoples, it is the sweetest and most sacred music on earth. Ruby was fortunate to have heard this sacred breath of Great Spirit. To others the singing sands is nothing more than a grand cacophony of noise. It all depends on who you are and your relationship with the desert. Don't wait for it and expect something to happen – it doesn't work like that. In fact, there are some folk that will never hear this desert music even if they've spent a whole lifetime listening for it. Hearing this sacred music of the desert had an immense impact on Ruby and the path that she finally chose to walk. She chose not to question or analyze this experience – she accepted it for what it was – something that made her stronger, resilient, and gave her personal power over her tragic past. She used this new-found power to do good, not only for herself, but for others. Time and time again she made an impact on those who lead desperate lives. It's as if Great Spirit called her to this quest. In closing I would just like to add that Ruby Broyles was like a desert blossom, dormant in the Winter of her life, and flowering into uncommon beauty in the Spring of her life. I will miss her deeply. And now let me introduce Tommy Broyles, Ruby's youngest son. He has some words for you."

Tommy stepped forward and held his mother's cane out in front of him, looked at it and then scanned the crowd.

"Thank you for the kind words about my mother, Souza. And thank you everyone for showing up to this special event."

Tommy's eyes got misty as he continued.

"Most of you had no idea that Ruby had any children. Souza and Pete were the only ones she confided in about her family back in Colorado. From what Souza told me she didn't talk about her past much. She was always concerned with looking ahead. When my father threw her out of our house years ago we lost contact with her. In subsequent years whenever I asked my father if he had heard about our mother's whereabouts, he would simply repeat: *She's probably on skid row somewhere, or drank herself to death in a flop house. Who cares?* I never really looked for my mother. I figured she didn't want to see us after what had happened. But I always wanted to know what became of her. Then one day I got that answer."

Tommy paused again, while leaning on the cane and rubbing his eyes with the other hand. He continued:

"Last year I received a letter from a lawyer in San Bernardino. She had hired him to track me down and send me this incredible long letter – sixty pages to be exact. After reading this letter it dawned on me just how profoundly my mother had changed. Growing up she was a woman who wanted power at any cost, and would step on others if they got in her way. This letter, however, presented a different person than I remembered. I now saw nothing but compassion and humility in her words. This past year I called her at least a dozen times and we exchanged several dozen emails. She wanted me to come and visit but I was managing a special project in Romania and couldn't get away. I did promise her however that I would visit as soon as the project ended."

Tommy paused again after Souza grabbed his shoulder and mumbled something in his ear. Both men smiled at one another.

"Five days ago, Souza emailed me about my mother's passing. I jumped on the first flight out of Romania and just got here yesterday afternoon. I can't express to you all how sad I feel right now. Last time I saw her was almost twenty years ago. Her last request was to have her ashes sprinkled at Monument Rock about two miles behind the motel. Early this morning at sunrise, Souza and me walked over there and did just that. My mother, Ruby Broyles, now belongs to the desert for eternity. And if by chance, one day you hear the Singing Sands, please think of her and what she accomplished with her life. If anyone else has something to say please step forward and give your name so I know who you are."

"Hello, Tommy. I'm Arturo from the Evangelista Family Law Center in San Bernardino. Both Pete and your mother were my clients over the years. As some of you know, Ruby came into some big money when Pete passed. The man had won the lottery before buying this motel, but never spent much of it. Ruby found herself sitting on over seven million dollars.

She completely refurbished and modernized the property with all the newest bells and whistles money can buy. But I think the important part here is the good she did with most of that cash. She set up a Charitable Trust to help victims and their families impacted by drunk drivers. She also set aside a special room here at the motel as a refuge for women who are fleeing domestic abuse.

Women can use the room for as long as they need it with all expenses paid by the motel. Twelve women have used this refuge over the years. Ruby was on a mission these last many years to give back to others anyway she could. I think she exceeded her goals with everything she did. I will miss that lady. She was one of a kind. That's all I have to say."

"Hi everyone. My name is Doris. Ruby and Pete gave me a second break at life after spending time in the joint. After Ruby brought me in to help manage things here we grew very close, because of the types of experiences we shared. Ruby was my best friend, almost a soul mate. She gave of herself one-hundred percent to others, even if they were strangers with nothing in common.

During the last four months of her illness she couldn't get around much without using her cane and dragging around that damn oxygen tank. Even when she initially received the news of her advanced lung cancer, she kept that wonderful smile on her face all the time, and always put the focus on the needs of others first and foremost. I still can't believe she's gone."

A slight build of a man, about mid-sixties, with longish gray hair and Van Dyke beard, stepped out of the crowd and started talking.

"I'm so sorry for your loss, Tommy. My name is Frank Darbe. I'm the editor of the local paper. Your mother and I were good friends these past fifteen years. We used to go on walks together to Monument Rock every weekend and talk about everything under the sun. This past year we didn't walk because of her health but we still maintained our weekly chat over pie and coffee. I would like to relate an unusual experience Ruby had with a dog many years ago.

About a month after Pete died, Ruby found an abandoned dog at Monument Rock. It was an older black Labrador with no collar or tags. It was simply circling the big rock like it was searching for something. It seemed well fed and there appeared to be no injuries. The odd thing about this dog, according to Ruby, is that it had a distinct odor of tobacco, sweat and Old Spice.

She took the dog back to the motel, gave it a bath and groomed it. That dog stayed by Ruby's side for the next three years, followed her everywhere, even slept on the foot of her bed. I'm sure some of you still remember that mutt. She called him Pete.

She later told me that she considered that mutt her guardian angel, because she was going through some tough times and wanting to drink again. But every time she had the urge, that mutt seem to come out of nowhere and give her this incredible look, that pierced her very being.

And when it seemed like the rough times were over, that mutt simply vanished one afternoon, never to be seen again. Ruby looked high and low, and even went back to Monument Rock many times, but knew deep down that it was gone for good.

After the disappearance of that mutt, life just got better and better for Ruby. She would be celebrating fifteen years of total and continuous sobriety this month. She kept an empty bottle of Russian vodka on her bedside table, with a plastic red rose stuck in it, to remind herself what could have been."

A few more people spoke briefly about knowing Ruby and experiences they had, and how she impacted their day-to-day lives for the better. The crowd finally sauntered away, talking among themselves, while going back to work or whatever they had been doing before the service.

Tommy, Souza, Frank, and most of the motel residents went inside the café to have pie and coffee and just visit. For this special occasion, Doris made Ruby's favorite pie which had been dubbed the *Ruby Red*.

Ruby had experimented for months just to get the rhubarb, strawberry and black cherry combination just right, and finally it became a huge hit with the motel residents and visitors. In fact, Souza had entered it in the San Bernardino county pie bake-off competition, and it won Ruby the first-place ribbon.

When they were all settled and enjoying their pie, Souza turned to Tommy and said:

"Well Tommy, have you thought about what I said this morning on our walk to the big rock?"
Tommy put his coffee cup down and looked straight ahead, blinking several times before answering.

"I realize I'm the legal owner of this place now, but I also have responsibilities to my current employer. But it sure would be nice to continue what my mother started here. And it would be even better to get away from that high-pressured oil refinery work I do."

Souza peered into Tommy's eyes and gave him a big wink and said:

"All I ask is that you sleep on it and look at it from every angle, and then imagine how it will affect the rest of your days. Maybe, just maybe, this is something you've been looking for all your life and just didn't know it. Take another walk over to the big rock. Maybe talk it over with Ruby. You'll find your answer."

Tommy rubbed his eyes and looked at the ceiling.

"Okay, you win. I'll think it over. I'll spend a couple more days here and let you know."

Doris walked over to where Souza and Tommy were sitting and re-filled their coffee cups. Tommy looked intensely at Doris for a moment, causing her to fidget.

"Is there something else you wanted Mr. Broyles?"

"Yeah. Just before my mother passed, she told me all about you. How you endured those years of abuse and incarceration, and what great friends you had become. You know, she thought very highly of you." Tommy glanced at Souza and then back at Doris.

"Whether I decide to stay or leave, I don't have a clue about running a place like this. I wouldn't know where to begin. How would you feel if I offered you the job of managing this property for me? The room and board would be free plus a monthly salary of $3300."

"I would be grateful to accept your offer."

"Excellent. What my mother said about you speaks volumes about your character. You would be the perfect successor to her legacy."

Doris extended her hand to Tommy and gave him a hearty handshake. Souza directed his attention to Tommy and said:

"Ruby would have liked this the way things are turning out. And if you decide to stay, Doris here is a great teacher. She can show you how to use a skill saw like a seasoned professional as well as about integrity and life in general."

Souza gave them both a big wink and smile.

FINIS

Afterward

The inspiration for this story came from my first visit to the small town of Lucerne Valley, California in the summer of 1980. Yes, folks, it is a real place just as I described it in the story. I spent the night at the Ace Motel which became the template for the Roach Motel & café. I also dined at the delicatessen located inside the Lucerne Valley Market, which seemed like the social hub of this tiny, dusty community.

However, the Chemehuevi Community Center is a complete figment of my imagination. But I did have a rather interesting one hour conversation with two Chemehuevi Native People inside the market. This is where my fascination with Chemehuevi culture was born.

The books, journals, academic papers, and conversations with nearly a dozen Chemehuevi Native People over the years, became an excellent resource on native culture and spirituality in preparing this story. The character of Souza Maynard is a composite of several male Chemehuevi people who I came to know over the years.

It is from these folks that I learned about the rampant and deadly scourge of alcoholism among Native Peoples. My debt to the Chemehuevi Native Peoples and their culture is enormous. The discussion about alcoholism in my story is not to be construed as an endorsement or approval of Alcoholics Anonymous. However, I wholeheartedly endorse and support total sobriety for those individuals that need it to keep on living among the rest of us – however they may achieve that goal.

This is not just an interesting, compelling story or a review of the life and times of a certain character. I had an agenda early on when creating this story. The form of the **novelette** – which is not used much in this modern age – seemed the perfect vehicle for my story. The novelette form is often written as a satirical, moral or educational nature and purpose, and typically focuses on one main character.

Examples in literature of this form come to mind: Hermann Hesse's *Knulp*; Russell Banks' *The Relation of My Imprisonment*; Saul Bellow's *Seize The Day*; and Elie Wiesal's *Dawn*.

In September 2015, I visited Lucerne Valley again to do some last-minute research and take dozens of pictures. Somethings changed radically while others stayed the same as before. The Ace Motel has been closed for over ten years and completely abandoned by the owners. The Lucerne Valley Market & Deli is still the hub of the community, but it just didn't have that romantic feel I experienced decades earlier.

While walking about the store however, I noticed a group of young Chemehuevi men buying several 24-can cubes of Budlight beer. And while there a major rainstorm moved through the area, causing flash flooding, which prevented me from driving over to the Big Rock. The Y Saloon, which also played a role in my story, closed in the Spring of 2015.

About the Author

I am a 62-year-old grumpy white guy with an attitude the size of the Grand Canyon and a sense of wonder as big as the Milky Way galaxy. My cultural interests include Celtic folk music, the old English comedies on BBC America, foreign films (especially by Akira Kurosawa & Werner Herzog), and the theater.

I read many magazines and journals, including: Free Inquiry, Atlantic Monthly, The Linux Journal, Martha Stewart Living, Food & Wine, Sky & Telescope, and of course, the New York Review of Books.

My hobbies are few. For the past 44 years I have been an affection ado of Homeric literature. In my humble opinion, the Iliad & Odyssey are the greatest examples of heroic-epic writing ever produced by the human race.

Of all the translations of Homer I've read down through the years, the translation by Alexander Pope is by far my favorite. I have read nearly one-hundred scholarly books about Homer and his times, since my passion was ignited by an English teacher, Ms. Dorothy Buckley, at Hayward High school in California. I re-read the Homeric classics at least every seven years and it never gets boring.

For the past 29 years, I have been living in the Concordia neighborhood, of Northeast Portland, Oregon. And since my early retirement in February 2016, I have had more time to write the stories, poems and essays to amuse myself and others. My five cats, three dogs and domestic partner are my biggest cheer leaders and fans. If you wish to keep abreast of my writing projects, please see the links below:

My Amazon Author Page
www.amazon.com/author/benjamindouglass

The American Poet
www.bendouglasspdx.com

Google Plus Social Network
www.google,com/+BenDouglassAuthorPDX

Addendum

I hope you enjoyed this short novel – it is my first. If you did, I would be very grateful if you write a review on Amazon. The review can be one sentence long, and it can be good, bad or indifferent. The important thing is the review itself. ***Independent self-published authors*** don't have the resources of the big publishing houses. We rely on our readers to promote our books by posting reviews. Please locate the book title on my Amazon Author Page:

www.amazon.com/author/benjamindouglass

NOTES

NOTES

CPSIA information can be obtained
at www.ICGtesting.com
Printed in the USA
LVHW031339010321
680268LV00033B/792

9 781537 082707